DEMCO

If I Were the Wind

By **Lezlie Evans**

Illustrated by
Victoria Lisi

Ideals Children's Books • Nashville, Tennessee
an imprint of Hambleton-Hill Publishing, Inc.

For my mother, Julie Peterson, with love.
                                   —L. E.

With love to my mother and daughter.
And special thanks to Kaitlyn.
                                   —V. L.

Text copyright © 1997 by Lezlie Evans
Illustrations copyright © 1997 by Hambleton-Hill Publishing, Inc.

Published by Ideals Children's Books
An imprint of Hambleton-Hill Publishing, Inc.
Nashville, Tennessee 37218

Printed and bound in Mexico

Library of Congress Cataloging-in-Publication Data
Evans, Lezlie.
    If I were the wind / by Lezlie Evans ; illustrated by Victoria
Lisi.
        p.   cm.
    Summary: A mother offers reassurances that no matter what
outlandish event were to happen, she would always find a way to take
care of her beloved child.
    ISBN 1-57102-096-9
    [1. Mother and child—Fiction. 2. Stories in rhyme.] I. Lisi,
Victoria, ill. II. Title.
PZ8.3.E915If   1997
[E]—dc20   96-38639
                                                               CIP
                                                                AC

The illustrations in this book were rendered in watercolor.
The text type was set in Cochin.
The display type was set in Biorst.
Color separations were made by Color 4, Inc.
Printed and bound by R.R. Donnelley & Sons Company.

First Edition

10 9 8 7 6 5 4 3 2 1

"Mother?" asked the child, climbing up on her knee.
"If you could be anything, what would you be?"

"I'd be your mother," she said with a smile.

The child smiled back and then thought for a while.

"If you could do anything, what would you do?"

"Oh, that's easy, my child. I'd take care of you."

"But what if a witch came along one day,
and that wicked old witch she stole you away
and changed you into the wind, or a tree?

"Or maybe a coat,
or a boat,
or the sea?
Mother, how would you take care of me?"

"If I were the wind I would dry all your tears.

"If I were a lock I would lock up your fears.

"If I were a coat I'd protect you from cold.
With pockets and zippers, your treasures I'd hold.

"If I were a book I would tell you a tale.
If I were a boat then together we'd sail.

"If I were the sun I would color your sky,
with crimson and scarlet to dazzle your eye.

"If I were the sea in my waves you could play.
If I were a path I would show you the way.

"If I were a tree in my shade you could lie;
together we'd watch as white clouds floated by.

"If I were a box all your toys I would keep.
If I were a song I would sing you to sleep.

"If I were a chair I would rock you all day,
    and on my soft cushion your head you could lay.

"If I were a fire, for you I'd burn bright.
If I were the moon I would watch you all night.

"If I were a quilt I would wrap you up tight,
and take you to dreamland to play for the night.

"I'll love you forever, not just for a day,
and there's no wicked witch to take me away.
I won't be the wind, or a boat, or the sea.
I won't be a box, nor a chair, nor a tree.

"So hush now, my child, and I'll hold you tight,
and we'll go to dreamland to play for the night."